Licensed exclusively to Top That Publishing Ltd
Tide Mill Way, Woodbridge, Suffolk, IP12 1AP, UK
www.topthatpublishing.com
Text copyright © 2011 Tide Mill Media
Illustration copyright © 2011 Dubravka Kolanovic
All rights reserved
0 2 4 6 8 9 7 5 3 1
Manufactured in China

Written by Eilidh Rose
Illustrated by Dubravka Kolanovic

ISBN 978-1-84956-440-3

A catalogue record for this book is available from the British Library

# Little Penguin
## Learns to Swim

Written by Eilidh Rose

Illustrated by Dubravka Kolanovic

It was an important day for Little Penguin.
He was going swimming for the very first time.

Little Penguin was nervous about learning to swim,
but he wanted to splash and play with his friends.
So he started to slowly waddle along the icy
path towards the big, blue ocean.

Little Penguin was shuffling through the snow, practising flapping his flippers and wiggling his feet, when he saw Little Bird hopping towards him.

'I'm learning to fly!' said Little Bird.

'Are you scared?' asked Little Penguin.

'Not really. I'm not very good yet, but I can almost get off the ground,' said Little Bird proudly.

Little Penguin continued down the icy path to the ocean. Suddenly, he saw a black shadow on the fluffy white snow. High above him in the bright blue sky was Little Bird, twirling and swooping through the air.

'I'm finally flying!' Little Bird squawked happily.

As he was practising wiggling his feet,
Little Penguin heard a splash and Little Seal
jumped up on the ice beside him.

'I'm learning to fish!'
said Little Seal, happily.

'Are you nervous?' asked Little Penguin.

'Not really. I haven't caught anything yet, but it's lots of fun!'

Little Seal saw a school of fish swimming past, so she quickly plunged back into the water.

Waddling on, Little Penguin heard
a big splash and an excited shout.

'Look, Little Penguin!'
cried Little Seal. 'I caught a fish!'
Little Seal whizzed off to show all of her other friends.

Little Penguin felt tired
so he sat down for a rest.
As he was sitting on the ice,
a big wave splashed him.

'Sorry, Little Penguin,' said Little Whale.
'I'm learning to jump.'

'Are you scared?' asked Little Penguin.

'Not really. So far I've only done bellyflops,
but I can almost get high enough for
big jumps,' said Little Whale,
weaving through the waves.

As Little Penguin got to his feet and shuffled on,
he saw a shape jumping high above him.
It was Little Whale, leaping above the waves!

'Look at this one!' cried Little Whale,
somersaulting through the air.

Little Penguin was still worrying about
how to flap his flippers and wiggle his feet.
He could see all of his friends splashing and
sliding into the water, playing lots of fun games.

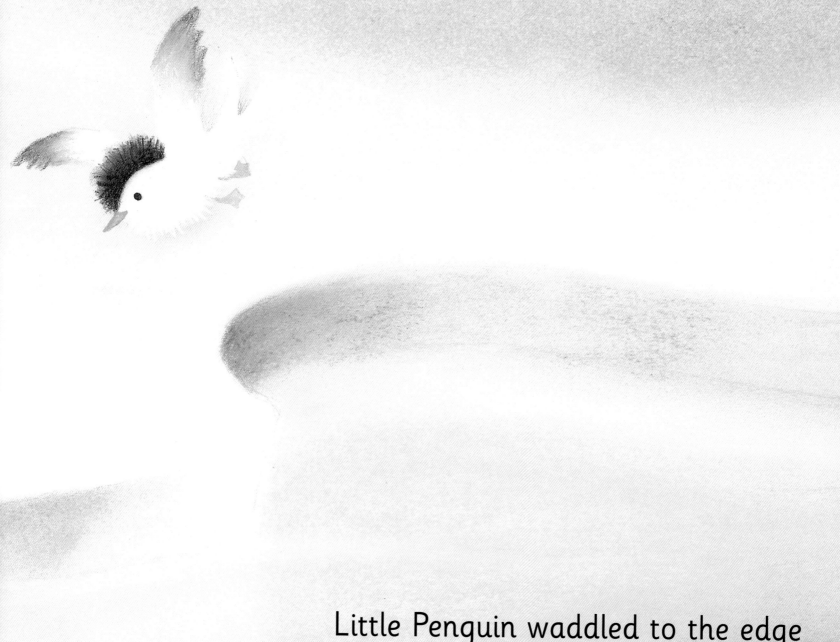

Little Penguin waddled to the edge
and looked down into the deep, dark water.
It looked very cold and he didn't want to go in.
But then he thought about his friends and how
they were not scared to learn new things.

Little Penguin shuffled closer and,
with a deep breath, slid on his
tummy and slipped easily into the water.
Just like he had practised, Little Penguin
flapped his flippers and wiggled his feet,
twirling and twisting through the water.

Little Penguin whizzed over to his
friends to join in with their games.
Even though he had been nervous before,
Little Penguin could not wait to come
back for more fun tomorrow!